THUMBELINA
By Hans Christian Andersen
Translated from the original Danish text by Marlee Alex
Illustrated by Toril Marö Henrichsen
Published by Scandinavia Publishing House,
Nørregade 32, DK-1165 Copenhagen; Denmark
Text:© Copyright 1984 Scandinavia Publishing House
Artwork:© Copyright 1984 Toril Marö Henrichsen and
Scandinavia Publishing House
Printed in Italy

ISBN 0 8317-8777-5

Thumbelina

Hans Christian Andersen
Illustrated by Toril Marö Henrichsen

GALLERY BOOKS
An Imprint of W. H. Smith Publishers Inc.
112 Madison Avenue
New York City 10016

There once was a woman who desperately wanted a little child. But as she did not know where she could get one from she went to an old witch and said: "I would so love to have a tiny child. Won't you please tell me where I could get one?" "Yeeesss. We should be able to do something about that!" said the witch. "Here is a grain of barley. It is not the kind that grows in the fields, or that which is fed to the hens. Plant it in a flower pot and then watch what happens!"

"Thank you very much!" said the woman. She gave the witch 12 shillings, then went home and planted the grain of barley. Immediately a pretty flower sprang up which looked like a tulip bud. "What a pretty flower!" said the woman as she kissed the beautiful bud of red and yellow petals. Just as she did so, the flower burst open. Right in the middle of it, on the green pistil, sat a tiny girl. She was very lovely, and she was no longer than your thumb. Therefore the woman called her Thumbelina.

Her bed was made from at walnut shell. The mattress was made of blue violet petals, and the blanket was a soft rose petal. The woman set it on her table. Beside it she sat a bowl of water surrounded by flowers. On the water floated a large tulip petal, and here Thumbelina sat during the day and rowed from one side of the bowl to the other using two white horse hairs as oars. It was a most beautiful sight. She could sing as well; as delicately and sweetly as you have ever heard.

One night as Thumbelina lay in her walnut shell bed, a hideous toad hopped in the window through a broken window pane. The ugly, fat and slimy toad hopped right down onto the table where Thumbelina was asleep under the red rose petal.

"She would make a nice wife for my son!" said the toad as she grabbed the walnut shell with the sleeping Thumbelina inside. And away she hopped through the window pane and down into the garden.

Nearby ran a large wide creek. Beside the bank was a muddy marsh where the toad lived with her son. Ugh! He was as ugly and horrible as his mother. "Rivet, rivet, rekkeke-kex!" was all he could say when he saw the pretty little girl in the walnut shell.

"Quiet! She might wake up!" said the old toad. "Let's set her out on the water on a lily pad. It will seem like an island to her. Then she won't try to get away from us while we prepare the room down under the mud where you two will live."

In the creek grew many water lilies and their big green leaves floated on the water. The old toad swam out to the largest leaf which was furthest out, and she sat the walnut shell holding Thumbelina on it.

The poor little girl woke up quite early the next morning and when she saw where she was, Thumbelina began to cry bitterly for she was surrounded by water and could't reach the shore at all. The old toad was busy down in the mud decorating her house with rushes and yellow flowers. She wanted it to be neat and tidy for her new daughter-in-law. Then she swam with her ugly son out to fetch Thumbelina's little bed, which was to be set up in the bridal chamber before Thumbelina herself arrived. The old toad curtsied before Thumbelina and said, "This is my son. He will be your husband, and the two of you will be cosy down in the mud!"

"Rivet, rivet, rekke-ke-kex!" was all the son could say.

Then they took the elegant little bed and swam away with it, leaving Thumbelina sitting all alone crying on the green lily pad. She didn't want to live in the house of the ugly toad, or have her hideous son for a husband.

The small fish swimming in the water had seen the toad and heard what she had said. So they stuck their heads up to see the little girl. As soon as they set eyes on her, they knew she was too pretty to live with the ugly toad and they vowed not to let it happen! They flocked around the stem of the lily pad upon which she stood, and nibbled at it until it broke free. The leaf floated down the creek with Thumbelina, far away where the toad couldn't reach her. Thumbelina sailed past many different places. The small birds in the bushes saw her and sang "Such a lovely little maid!" The leaf floated further and further away, and so Thumbelina travelled into another land.

A little white butterfly fluttered about her and finally sat down on the leaf. It liked Thumbelina, and Thumbelina was happy because the toad could no longer reach her, and because everything she sailed past was so beautiful. The sun shone on the water and looked just like shimmering gold. Thumbelina took her sash, bound one end around the butterfly and the other end around the stem of the leaf. The leaf began to move much faster as the butterfly flew down the river. Just then a large beetle came flying down. Seeing Thumbelina, he clutched her around her tiny waist and flew up into a tree with her. The green leaf sailed down the creek, and the poor butterfly flew with it, for he was tied to the leaf and could not break loose.

Goodness, how frightened poor little Thumbelina was when the beetle flew up into the tree with her. But she grieved for the beautiful white butterfly she had tied to the leaf. If he could not free himself, he would starve to death.

The beetle landed with Thumbelina on the biggest, greenest leaf of the tree, gave her a sweet flower to eat and told her that she was most charming, even though she didn't look at all like a beetle.

Later, all the other beetles who lived in that tree came by to visit. They looked at Thumbelina, and the young lady-beetles said: "She only has two legs, how awful!" "She has no antennas! She looks like a human! How ugly!" said all the other female beetles. Really they thought Thumbelina was very lovely and secretly they were jealous of her beauty.

The beetle who had taken Thumbelina also thought she was very lovely. But when all the others said she was hideous, he began to think so too, and decided he wouldn't keep her after all. He decided to let her go, so he flew her down out of the tree and set her down on a camomile flower. Thumbelina cried because she thought she was so ugly that even the beetle didn't want her, but she was the loveliest girl you can imagine, as delicate and bright as the prettiest rose petal.

11

Throughout the summer, poor Thumbelina lived all alone in the great forest. She made a bed of grass for herself and hang it under a large dock leaf so it was sheltered from the rain. She picked the sweetest flowers from which she ate the nectar and drank the morning dew. Summer and autumn passed, and winter came; the long, cold winter. All the birds who had sang so beautifully for her flew away for winter. The trees and the flowers withered, and the large leaf under which she lived curled up into a yellow dried stalk. Thumbelina was dreadfully cold, for her clothes were in rags, and she herself was delicate and tiny. Poor Thumbelina would freeze to death! Soon it began to snow. Every snowflake that fell on her felt like a whole shovelful because she was, as you know, only as long as your thumb. She wrapped herself into a withered leaf, but it couldn't keep her warm. She shivered in the cold.

Close beside the forest was a large corn field. The corn had long since been harvested and only the bare dry stubble stuck out of the frozen earth. It seemed like a forest to the shivering Thumbelina. As she walked across the field, she came to a fieldmouse's door. It was a little hole down under the corn stalkes. The fieldmouse lived there all warm and cosy. Her living room was full of grain, and she had a nice kitchen and dining room. Poor little Thumbelina sat down outside the door like a common beggar girl, and asked for a little piece of grain as she hadn't had anything to eat in two days. "You poor little thing!" said the fieldmouse, who was a good-hearted mouse. "Come into my warm parlour and eat with me!" As they ate she became very fond of Thumbelina and said, "You are most welcome to stay with me this winter, but you must keep my parlour tidy and tell me stories, for I do love stories!" And Thumbelina did whatever the kindhearted fieldmouse asked, and she was well looked after.

Soon we'll be having a visitor!" said the fieldmouse. "My neighbour visits me every week. He is even richer than I am. He has big rooms and a beautiful black velvet fur coat. If you could get him for your husband, then you would be well looked after. But he is blind, so you must tell him the loveliest stories you know!"

But Thumbelina was not the least bit interested, and she didn't want the neighbour for a husband, for he was a mole. He came and made his visit in his black fur coat. The fieldmouse said he was very rich and learned, and that his house was twenty times larger than hers. But he hated the sun and the beautiful flowers. He spoke ill of them for he had never seen them. But Thumbelina sang "Twinkle, Twinkle Little Star" and "Ring Around the Roses" so sweetly for him that he fell in love with her. But he didn't say anything for he was a very reserved fellow. The mole had recently dug a long tunnel through the earth from his house to the house of the fieldmouse, and the fieldmouse and Thumbelina could take walks there whenever they wanted. But he warned them not to be afraid of the dead bird which lay in the tunnel. It must have died only very recently when the winter began, and now just lay where the mole had made his passageway.

The mole took a piece of dry rotten wood which shines like fire in the long, dark tunnel. When they came to where the dead bird lay, the mole pushed a big hole in the roof so that the light could shine through. In the middle of the floor lay the dead swallow, with its beautiful wings against its sides. The poor bird had surely frozen to death. Thumbelina felt so sorry for it. She loved all small birds, for they had sung for her during the summer. But the mole shoved it with his short legs and said: 'We won't hear a single peep from this one again! How disgusting to be born a bird. Thank heavens none of my children ever will be. He has nothing but his chirp and then is bound to starve to death in the winter!" "Yes, a sensible man like you can just as well say it." said the fieldmouse. "What does a bird gain by all its chirping when the winter comes?"

Thumbelina didn't say anything, but when the other two had turned their backs to the bird she bent down, parted the feathers that lay over its head and kissed it on its closed eye. "Maybe it was this very one that sang so sweetly for me this summer," she thought. "It made me so happy, that dear, beautiful bird."

The mole closed up the hole in the roof and escorted the ladies home. That night Tumbelina couldn't sleep. She got up, made a large, lovely blanket of hay, and carried it down to spread over the dead bird. She laid soft cotton, which she had found in the living room, around the bird so it would not be on the cold earth.

"Goodbye, you beautiful little bird!" she said.
"Goodbye and thank you for your beautiful little songs this summer when all the trees were green and the sun shone so warmly on both of us." Then she laid her head upon the bird's chest. It sounded as if something was beating inside. It was the bird's heart. The bird wasn't dead; it lay in a coma and the warmth had brought life back to it.

Thumbelina trembled with fright, because the bird was much bigger than she was. But she gathered her courage, laid the cotton closer around the poor swallow and fetched a mint leaf, which she herself used as a blanket, to lay over its head.

The following night she quietly crept down to it again, and saw that it was indeed recovering. It opened its eyes for an instant and saw Thumbelina. "Thank you kindly, you pretty little child!" said the sick swallow." I have been warmed up very nicely. Soon I'll be strong enough to fly again in the warm sunshine." "Oh," Thumbelina answered, "it's cold outside. It's snowing and you would freeze. Stay in your bed, I'll take good care of you."

Thumbelina brought the swallow water in a flower petal. He drank it and told her how he had torn one of his wings on a thornbush, so he couldn't fly as fast as the other swallows. They had flown far, far away to warmer lands, but he had finally fallen to earth. He couldn't remember any more of what happened or how he came to be where he was.

The swallow stayed in the tunnel all through the winter. Thumbelina was good to him, and nursed him back to health. She told neither the mole nor the fieldmouse anything about him, because she knew they didn't like the poor little swallow.

As soon as spring arrived, and the sun warmed the earth, the swallow said goodbye to Thumbelina. She opened the hole above him as the mole had done. The sun shone in, and the swallow asked her to come with him. He said that she could sit on his back and they could fly together out into the green forest. But Thumbelina knew it would make the fieldmouse sad if she left suddenly. "No." said Thumbelina. "I cannot go." "Farewell! Farewell! You good, sweet girl!" said the swallow as he flew out into the sunshine. Thumbelina watched with tears in her eyes, for she had grown to love the swallow.

"Twe-eet, twe-eet!" sang the bird as he flew into the green forest. Thumbelina became very sad, for she wasn't allowed to go outside into the warm sunshine. The grain sown in the field over the fieldmouse's house grew tall and became a dense forest, shading the house and the doorway.

"This summer, you must prepare your trousseau!" said the fieldmouse to Thumbelina, for the dreary mole next door in the black velvet fur coat had proposed to her. "You will need both woollens and linen! You will need chair coverings and bed coverings when you become the mole's wife!" Thumbelina had to spin thread and yarn. The fieldmouse hired four spiders to weave both day and night. The mole visited each evening and he always talked about how glad he would be when the summer was over and the sun wasn't so hot, nor the earth so hard.

Yes, when the summer was over then the wedding would be held. But Thumbelina wasn't at all pleased for she didn't love the boring old mole. Every morning when the sun rose, and every evening when it set, she would think of how light and beautiful it was out there. She wished desperately that she could see the dear swallow again. But he never came. He had flown away into the green forest.

When autumn arrived, Thumbelina's trousseau was finished. "In four weeks, you will be married!" said the fieldmouse to her. Thumbelina cried and said she didn't want to marry that dreary mole.
"Nonsense!" said the fieldmouse. "Don't be contrary, or I'll bite you! You are getting a very good husband. Even the queen hasn't a fur coat like his! He has a well stocked kitchen and cellar! You should thank the heavens above for him!"
The day of the wedding arrived and the mole came to fetch Thumbelina. She would now have to live with him deep under the ground, never to come out into the warm sunshine again. The poor child was so unhappy at the prospect of saying goodbye to the beautiful sun. She had at least had permission to see it from the doorway of the fieldmouse's house.
"Goodbye, beautiful, bright sunshine!" she called as she stretched out her arms into the air and took a few steps outside the door. The grain had now been harvested and only the dry stubble was left on the field. "Goodbye, goodbye!" she said as she hugged a little red flower standing there. "Please greet the dear swallow from me if you see him!"

"Twe-eet, twe-eet!" There was a familiar sound above her. As she looked up she saw the swallow flying by. He saw Thumbelina and was overjoyed. She told him how sorry she was because she was to be married to the ugly mole and would live deep under the ground where the sun never shines. She couldn't help crying as she spoke.

"The cold winter is on it's way," said the swallow. "I am going to fly far away to the warmer lands. Do you want to come with me? You can sit on my back! If you tie yourself securely with your sash, we will fly away from the ugly mole and his gloomy rooms: far away, over the mountains where the sun shines more beautifully than here, where it is always summer and where there are lovely flowers all year round. Fly with me, sweet little Thumbelina. You saved my life when I lay frozen in the dark earth."

"Yes, I want to go with you!" said Thumbelina. And so she climbed up on the bird's back and put her feet on his broad wings. She tied her sash to one of his strongest feathers and flew up with him into the air over forest and sea; high up over the mountains which are always covered with snow. Thumbelina was freezing in the cold air until she snuggled beneath the bird's warm feathers. She left only her little head exposed so that she could see all the beauty below.

At last they arrived in the warm lands. The sun shone bright and along the ditches and slopes grew the loveliest blue and green grapes. Lemons and oranges grew in the orchards, and the fragrance of myrtle and mint hung in the air. Along the country roads, little children ran and played with big colourful butterflies. But the swallow flew even further. Everything became more and more beautiful. Under green trees and by a blue sea stood an ancient castle of shining, white marble. Vines wound their way up around the tall pillars. On top of the pillars were many swallow's nests, and in one of them lived the swallow who had carried Thumbelina.

"Here is my house!" said the swallow. "You choose for yourself one of the pretty flowers growing below where you can live!" "How wonderful!" cried Thumbelina and clapped her tiny hands. One of the marble pillars had fallen to the earth and broken into three pieces, and between the cracks grew beautiful, large white flowers. The swallow flew down with Thumbelina and set her on one of the petals. How amazed she was! A little man sat in the middle of the flower. He was as white and transparent as if he were made of glass. He had a pretty golden crown on his head and beautiful bright wings on his shoulders. He wasn't much larger than Thumbelina herself. He was the guardian angel of the flowers. In every flower lived such a little man or little lady, but this one was the king over them all.
"Goodness, isn't he handsome!" whispered Thumbelina to the swallow.

The little king had been frightened by the swallow who was much larger than he, but when he saw Thumbelina, he was enchanted. She was the most charming young lady he had ever seen. He took off his golden crown and set it on her head. Then he asked what her name was and if she would be his wife and become queen over all the flowers!

Yes, here was indeed a man who was different to the toad's son and the mole with the black fur coat. So Thumbelina said yes to the courteous little king. Then a tiny lady or gentleman stepped out of each flower. They were as bright as stars, and each of them brought Thumbelina a present. The nicest of all was an exquisite pair of white wings. They were placed on her back so that she could also fly from flower to flower.

Everyone was happy. The swallow sat on his nest and sang for them as well as he could, but in his heart he felt such sadness. For he loved Thumbelina and never wanted to be separated from her. "You shall not be called Thumbelina any longer!" said the angel of the flowers. "It is an ugly name, and you are so beautiful. We will call you May!" "Farewell, farewell!" said the swallow as he flew away from the warm lands again; far away, back to Denmark. He had a little nest there by the window of the man who told this story. For the swallow sang for him, "Twe-eet, twe-eet!" And that is how we know what happened.